The Adventures of Benny and Watch

A PRESENT FOR GRANDFATHER

Created by **Gertrude Chandler Warner**

Illustrated by **Daniel Mark Duffy**

Albert Whitman & Company

Morton Grove, Illinois

You will also want to read:

Meet the Boxcar Children

Benny's New Friend

The Magic Show Mystery

Benny Goes Into Business

Watch Runs Away

The Secret Under the Tree

Benny's Saturday Surprise

Sam Makes Trouble

Watch, the Superdog!

Library of Congress Cataloging-in-Publication Data

Warner, Gertrude Chandler, 1890-1979
A present for Grandfather / created by Gertrude Chandler Warner;
illustrated by Daniel Mark Duffy.
p.   cm.
Summary: Benny wants to get something special for his grandfather's birthday, but
he has trouble finding the right present while trying to keep an eye on his dog Watch.
ISBN 0-8075-6625-X
[1. Grandfathers—Fiction. 2. Birthdays—Fiction. 3.Gifts—Fiction.]
I. Duffy, Daniel M., ill. II. Title.
PZ7.W244Pr   1998
[Fic]--dc21   98-6219
CIP
AC

The Boxcar Children

Henry, Jessie, Violet, and Benny Alden are orphans. They are supposed to live with their grandfather, but they have heard that he is mean. So the children run away and live in an old red boxcar. They find a dog, and Benny names him Watch.

When Grandfather finds them, the children see that he is not mean at all. They happily go to live with him. And, as a surprise, Grandfather brings the boxcar along!

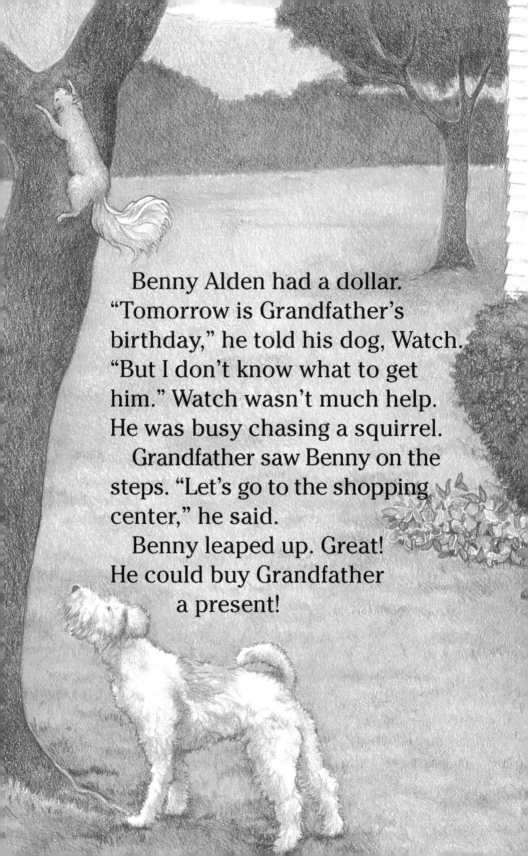

Benny Alden had a dollar. "Tomorrow is Grandfather's birthday," he told his dog, Watch. "But I don't know what to get him." Watch wasn't much help. He was busy chasing a squirrel.

Grandfather saw Benny on the steps. "Let's go to the shopping center," he said.

Benny leaped up. Great! He could buy Grandfather a present!

As they drove down the street,
Benny said, "There's Michael.
Can he come, too?" Michael was
Benny's friend. Michael asked his
mother and was back in a flash.

Al's Barbershop

Greenfield Bank

The *Better* Bakery

Grandfather parked the car in front of the shopping center. There was a barbershop, a bank, a bakery, and a gift shop on one of the blocks.

"I need a haircut," said Grandfather.

"We'll be in the gift shop," Benny said.

Benny, Michael, and Watch
went inside. The shop was filled with
fancy statues. Watch wagged his tail. A glass
cat was knocked off a shelf. Luckily, Benny
caught it just in time.

The woman behind the counter
said sternly, "No dogs allowed."

Benny took Watch outside.
"Wait here," he said.

Back inside, he saw a brass pen set. "That's neat," said Michael.

"It would look nice on Grandfather's desk," Benny agreed. Then he saw the price tag. "Twenty dollars! I only have one dollar!"

A furry blur hopped up and down outside the window. The blur was Watch. "Watch doesn't like it out there," said Michael.

"I'll talk to him," said Benny. When he went outside, Watch ran down the sidewalk. Benny chased his dog. "We can't play now!" he scolded.

Benny took Watch back to the gift store. "Sit," he said. But Watch wouldn't sit.

Benny found a box for Watch to stand on. "Now you can see us."

Benny went into the store again.
Michael held out a key ring. "This
only costs one dollar," he said.

"It's not very special," Benny said. "But it's all I can afford." He reached into his pocket and pulled out . . . nothing! "My dollar!" he cried. "It's gone!"

"Where did it go?" asked Michael.

"Maybe I lost it when I was chasing Watch," Benny said. "We have to find it."

Watch jumped happily off the box. "Help us find my dollar," Benny told the dog. Watch put his nose to the ground.

"Can he smell it?" Michael asked.

Benny was excited. "Let's follow him!" They dashed after the dog.

Watch's nose led them to the
end of the block. But instead of
Benny's dollar, Watch found an
old sandwich.

The two boys sat on the curb.
Watch sat down, too.

"Grandfather's birthday won't
be very special now," Benny
said glumly.

The boys watched a man hang a sign on the bank door. Benny read the words out loud: "'The best things in life are free.' The bank must be giving away *money*!"

The best things
✦ in life ✦
are free.

Benny and Michael hurried
over. "Excuse me, mister," Benny
said. "How do I get my free
money?"

The man smiled. "Oh, no.
The bank isn't giving away money.
They're giving away calendars.
Sorry, boys."

No one was sorrier than Benny.
How could he go to Grandfather's party
without a present?
Then Benny heard a voice coming
from the bakery. It was Grandfather.

"I'd like a dozen rolls," said Grandfather.
"How about some chocolate muffins?"
asked the baker. "They're great for breakfast."
Grandfather laughed. "My breakfasts aren't
much fun."

Every morning Grandfather had juice and something called oat bran. It looked like sawdust to Benny. Not much fun at all.

Suddenly, Benny had an idea.

Grandfather came out and asked, "Are you boys ready?"

"Yes," said Benny. He had work to do.

At home Benny talked with
Mrs. McGregor, the Aldens'
housekeeper. She liked his plan.

Next he found his brother and
sisters. They thought Benny's
idea was good, too.

There was one more thing to do. Benny went into his room. He made a card and wrote his name on it. Watch added his paw print.

The next morning, the dining room was decorated for a party. "Happy birthday!" the Aldens cried when Grandfather walked in.

The children all gave him presents.

Benny handed his card to Grandfather. It said: "Dear Grandfather, your brekfust will be fun for a month. Love, Benny and Watch."

"What does this mean?" Grandfather asked Benny.

Benny grinned. "Every day, Watch and I will make a surprise for your breakfast!"

Mrs. McGregor brought in a cake.
"Here's the first surprise," she said.
"Birthday cake for breakfast!"
exclaimed Grandfather.

"No oat bran today!" Benny said.
Grandfather really liked his
present. Benny was glad. It didn't
matter that he had lost his dollar.
He would have fun thinking up new
breakfast surprises.

"What will I have tomorrow?" asked Grandfather.

Benny smiled. "You'll have to wait and see!"